MW01147338

Books by Paige Sleuth

Cozy Cat Caper Mystery Series:

Murder in Cherry Hills (Book 1)

Framed in Cherry Hills (Book 2)

Poisoned in Cherry Hills (Book 3)

Vanished in Cherry Hills (Book 4)

Shot in Cherry Hills (Book 5)

Strangled in Cherry Hills (Book 6)

Halloween in Cherry Hills (Book 7)

Stabbed in Cherry Hills (Book 8)

Thanksgiving in Cherry Hills (Book 9)

Frozen in Cherry Hills (Book 10)

Hit & Run in Cherry Hills (Book 11)

Christmas in Cherry Hills (Book 12)

Choked in Cherry Hills (Book 13)

Dropped Dead in Cherry Hills (Book 14)

Valentine's in Cherry Hills (Book 15)

Drowned in Cherry Hills (Book 16)

Orphaned in Cherry Hills (Book 17)

Fatal Fête in Cherry Hills (Book 18)

Arson in Cherry Hills (Book 19)

Overdosed in Cherry Hills (Book 20)

Trapped in Cherry Hills (Book 21)

Missing in Cherry Hills (Book 22)

Crash in Cherry Hills (Book 23)

Independence Day in Cherry Hills (Book 24)

Checked Out in Cherry Hills (Book 25)

Blackmail in Cherry Hills (Book 26)

Last Supper in Cherry Hills (Book 27)

Slain in Cherry Hills (Book 28)
Clean Kill in Cherry Hills (Book 29)
Targeted in Cherry Hills (Book 30)
Due or Die in Cherry Hills (Book 31)
Recalled in Cherry Hills (Book 32)
Arrested in Cherry Hills (Book 33)
Bad Blood in Cherry Hills (Book 34)

Psychic Poker Pro Mystery Series:
Murder in the Cards (Book 1)

VANISHED *in* CHERRY HILLS

PAIGE SLEUTH

ISBN: 1518810802
ISBN-13: 978-1518810800

Published by Marla Bradeen.

This book is a work of fiction. Names, characters, businesses, places, events, and incidents are either products of the author's imagination or used in a fictitious manner. Any resemblance to actual persons (living or dead), actual businesses, or actual events is purely coincidental.

CHAPTER ONE

"I want to find my mother," Katherine Harper said.

Andrew Milhone's hand stilled, the mashed potatoes he had been about to shovel into his mouth freezing in front of him.

Kat looked at a couple sitting on the other side of the restaurant to help steady herself. Her heart had revved up the moment she'd mentioned her mother, and she felt a little dizzy.

When Andrew still hadn't spoken after a long moment had passed, she turned back to him. "Did you hear me? I want to find my mother."

"I heard you."

She folded her hands in her lap. "I have to admit, I thought you'd be more surprised about me wanting to look for her after all these years."

He set down his fork. "I am surprised. I mean, I was expecting this, but I didn't expect you to just blurt it out like that on our first date."

She frowned. "It's our second date."

Andrew regarded her as if she'd announced she wanted to dance a jig on top of their table. "It's our first date. I would recall if we'd been out before."

She gaped at him. "We went to Jessie's Diner last week."

He waved his hand. "Drinking a couple milkshakes at Jessie's doesn't count."

She looked around to make sure the waitress wasn't anywhere nearby before hunching closer and whispering, "You kissed me before we left my apartment."

He grinned, his adorable dimples making an appearance. "I know. It was a pretty good kiss too."

Kat couldn't prevent the flush that crept up her cheeks. It *was* a good kiss. She couldn't argue with him there.

"But one kiss doesn't turn a visit to Jessie's into a proper date," Andrew continued.

Kat lifted up her wineglass and took a sip, considering his point. "No, but you footing the bill does. If it weren't a date, we would have gone dutch."

"You used your employee discount," he countered.

"So?" He opened his mouth but she held up her hand before he could say anything. "And we're getting off topic."

He pushed a hank of sandy hair off his forehead. "Right. You want to find your mother."

She nodded, the lighthearted intermission fading as rapidly as it had appeared. "I've been thinking about what you said last week, about how life is short and we only have so much time."

His eyes softened. "I remember."

She set her wineglass down, unable to hold it steady now that her hand had started shaking. "If I don't find her now, I'm afraid I'll never know what happened to make her abandon me. What if she dies before I get the chance to talk to her?"

Andrew covered one of her hands with his. "Have you considered that she might not be alive?"

Kat blanched. Although she'd given a fleeting thought to the idea, it had been too unpleasant to dwell on for very long.

"You can't rule out the possibility," Andrew

said softly. "Given her history."

Kat swallowed. "As a drug addict, you mean."

Andrew nodded.

She straightened. "Well, alive or not, I feel compelled to look for her. I have so many unanswered questions about my past, questions only she can answer. Growing up in foster care, it's like I always felt there was this huge hole in my life. She's the only one who can even come close to filling it. I don't want to spend forever always wondering if I should have looked for her or regretting that I never made an effort to reach out." She knew she was rambling and cut herself off with a deep breath.

"I don't want to talk you out of it. I just want you to be prepared for whatever we find."

She nodded, knowing he wasn't trying to be negative. As a police detective, she figured he was simply programmed to expect the worst.

Andrew squeezed her hand. "And I definitely want to help."

Although Kat knew he would, hearing his words lifted a huge weight from her shoulders. Still, she had no clue how to go about looking for a woman she didn't remember and hadn't seen in three decades.

"So, where do we start?" she asked, hoping

Andrew would know.

"We'll see what information we can dig up and go from there."

Kat nodded, her mind churning. "I could search around on the Internet."

"That would be wise. I know you're a computer whiz."

She rolled her eyes. "I'm not a whiz. I'm just more comfortable with them than you are."

He grinned. "Right."

Kat picked up her fork and played with it, needing to do something with her hands. "Do you think she's still in Washington State?"

"Kat." Andrew looked into her eyes. "I'd just be speculating if I said anything."

She knew he was right, but her brain wouldn't rest. Despite spending most of her thirty-two years trying to forget about the woman who had given her life, now that she'd made the decision to track her down she felt an urgency that hadn't been there before.

Kat shifted in her seat, anxious to get moving. "When do you want to begin?"

Andrew motioned the waitress over. "As soon as I pay the bill."

CHAPTER TWO

Andrew walked Kat up to her apartment when they arrived back at her place. The September night was pleasant, with fall less than three weeks away. If she wasn't itching to begin her search she would have suggested a stroll around the neighborhood.

Typically Kat would have been nervous about a guy accompanying her upstairs after their second—or first—date, but at the moment she couldn't prevent the excitement that thrummed in her chest. She knew Andrew well enough to know he would be a complete gentleman. And, as much as she liked him, that was a good thing. Romance had completely fled her mind as soon as they'd started discussing her mother.

"You might be able to find a last known address online," Andrew was saying as they stepped out of the elevator and walked the distance to her unit. "That would give us a start."

"But I don't even know her name," Kat said, slipping her key in her door.

Andrew's brow furrowed. "I thought it was Maybelle Harper."

"*Was*, yes. That's what's written on my birth certificate, anyway. But what if she got married since then? She could be an Obama now."

Andrew's mouth twitched. "You think your mother is an Obama?"

Kat pushed her apartment door open. "She could be."

Andrew followed her inside. Tom, Kat's big, brown-and-black cat, ambled over to greet them. Matty, her other, more reserved yellow-and-brown tortoiseshell, didn't move from her resting spot on the couch.

"Hey, Tom," Andrew said, crouching down to pet the friendly feline. "What do you think about finding out you're the grandson of President Obama?"

Kat rolled her eyes as she shut the door. "I used that as an example."

She tossed her purse on the coffee table before wandering over to the couch and perching next to Matty. Matty allowed her chin to be scratched, although she made sure Kat knew she was merely tolerating the attention for her human's benefit.

Still rubbing Tom with one hand, Andrew reached over and plucked a picture off of Kat's coffee table. He studied it for a moment before looking up. "This is her?"

Kat nodded, her heart beating a little faster when she caught sight of her mother captured in the thirty-year-old Polaroid. "That's the only picture I have of her."

Andrew squinted at the photo. "You look like her."

His words surprised her. "Really?" She leaned over to peer at the photo. In it, her mother was smiling, her brown hair brushing the collar of her blouse as she struck a pose for the camera. "Other than our hair color, I don't see a resemblance."

"I can see it."

Tom dragged himself closer to Andrew, clearly unhappy about having his rubdown curtailed by an old picture. Andrew got the hint. He tossed the photo back on the coffee table and refocused on Tom.

"When's the last time you saw her?" Andrew asked.

Kat shrugged. "I must have been about two. I don't even remember her."

"That would mean she left Cherry Hills around 1985."

"That sounds about right." Kat jumped off the couch and rubbed her palms together. "So let's get to work on finding her."

Andrew stood up. "I'm ready."

Kat turned on the computer in the corner of the living room while Andrew dragged one of her kitchen chairs over. Tom watched them, the longing reflected in his eyes suggesting that he hadn't received nearly enough attention. Her heart melting, Kat went over to pick him up.

Andrew grinned. "You're spoiling him."

"I am not." Kat kissed the top of Tom's head as she took her seat. "You're not spoiled, are you?" she crooned.

Tom settled down in her lap, closed his eyes, and began purring.

Andrew sat down, looking smug. "I believe you just proved my point."

Kat defiantly ran her hand down Tom's back. "Tom is the type of cat who needs reassurance that he's wanted."

"And Matty isn't?"

"Matty's more independent. As far as I know, she's never been in foster care."

At the mention of foster care, Andrew's expression turned serious. "Have you thought about what you're going to say to her?"

Kat didn't have to ask who he was talking about. She felt the familiar ping in her chest that appeared whenever she thought about her mother. "No."

Andrew studied her for a long moment. "It's not always easy, you know," he said, shifting in his chair. "Reconnecting with a parent, that is."

Kat tilted her head. "Was it easy for you?"

Andrew lifted one shoulder. "Every time she came back, I had to get over my anger at her all over again."

The ache in Kat's chest expanded. She remembered how envious she felt whenever Andrew had visitation time with one of his parents back when they'd both been in foster care together. At the time, she hadn't really appreciated that he'd had his own issues to deal with. She only knew that his mother was around and hers wasn't.

Andrew propped his elbows on his knees and leaned closer. "You ever think about looking for your dad too?"

Kat scratched the bridge of Tom's nose as he pressed his face into her hand. "Not so much."

"Why's that?"

"For one thing, I don't think he's ever met me. The space for his name is blank on my birth certificate." She shrugged. "I guess that doesn't make him as real to me."

For another thing, she didn't feel strong enough to handle the thought of reestablishing contact with two parents only to find out neither one wanted her, but Kat didn't say this out loud. Some thoughts were just too depressing to voice.

Andrew ran one fingertip down her arm. "Maybe your mom can tell you something about him."

"Maybe." Kat straightened. "But first we have to find her."

Andrew jutted his chin toward the computer monitor, his eyes sparkling with amusement. "Then get to work."

Kat positioned her fingers over the keyboard, careful not to disturb Tom. Tom settled deeper into her lap. All the attention appeared to have put him in a kitty coma.

Matty, on the other hand, was wide-awake. As soon as the clack of Kat's typing reached her ears, she trotted over and jumped on top of the desk, heading straight for the keyboard.

Kat paused to gently push her away. "Not now, Matty."

The look on the feline's face told Kat exactly what she thought of taking orders. Then, as if to prove her authority in this household, Matty took two steps forward and planted her rear end smack-dab in the center of the keyboard.

Kat groaned. "Matty."

"I'll hold her," Andrew offered, standing up.

He scooped Matty off the desk and cradled her next to his chest. Matty struggled against him until he reclaimed his seat and set her in his lap. She glared at him for a second, then curled up and let him pet her, evidently deciding to make the most of her forced relocation.

Kat smiled. "Now who's spoiling whom?"

Andrew smirked. "I'm doing this for you. Now get to work."

Kat obeyed by pulling up Google and typing in her mother's name. Just seeing the words 'Maybelle Harper' written out caused her stomach to flutter. Part of her couldn't believe she was really doing this. She was actually going to find her mother.

Kat had done a few cursory searches over the years, never turning up anything before she gave up. The part of her that feared her mother wouldn't want to see her long-lost daughter seemed to have a knack for talking her out of looking too seriously.

This time felt different. She'd never dragged another person into her search efforts before. Even if Andrew was a fellow foster-care survivor and she knew he wouldn't pressure her if she changed her mind, somehow looping him in made backing out no longer seem like an option.

But after fifteen minutes of different Google searches that brought back nothing but dead ends, Kat was ready to give up for a reason other than fear.

"I can't find anything," she said, pounding on the keyboard to release some of her frustration.

Matty, evidently viewing her venting as an invitation, jumped off Andrew's lap and tiptoed over to the keyboard. She sat down on the space bar and peered at Kat, a smug look on her face as her tail swept over the keys.

Andrew set his hand on Kat's shoulder. "You could be right about her changing her name."

Kat flopped back into her chair, all of her earlier enthusiasm draining away. Right now, she didn't even care if Matty locked up her computer. "If she changed her name, how do I even begin to find her?"

"We could start by checking marriage records," Andrew suggested. "Those things are online nowadays."

Kat gripped the mouse, clinging to the slim hope he'd given her. "That's a good idea."

Matty shifted slightly, causing four different windows to spring up on the monitor behind her. Kat set her hands on Matty's haunches and pulled her to where she couldn't do any damage. She still recalled the last time Matty had 'helped' her on the computer. She had needed to perform a cold reboot.

"We might try the social media sites too," Andrew said. "Sometimes women list their maiden names with their Facebook profiles."

Kat nodded, letting go of Matty so she could pet Tom as he adjusted positions in her lap. Why hadn't she thought to check Facebook?

Andrew's lips thinned. "I hate to even bring this up, but we might want to look into death records too."

Kat's hand froze, prompting Tom to nudge it with his nose. She started stroking him again, but barely felt his fur gliding under her fingers.

"If your mother died, there should be a record of it somewhere," Andrew said.

Although Kat didn't want to entertain that possibility, she knew she had to. "I didn't find her obituary online. At least, I didn't find any obituaries linked to a Maybelle Harper."

"She might not have had an obituary."

A stone settled in Kat's stomach as she absorbed the implications of his words. What he meant, of course, was that perhaps nobody had cared enough about her mother to honor her memory with a printed tribute.

Andrew coughed. "But that's all speculation. We don't really know anything for sure, and we won't until we track down where she went after you last saw her in '85."

"Still, you're right," Kat said, unable to hide the glum tone in her voice. "She *could* be dead. I have to prepare myself for that."

Andrew didn't say anything. He just rested one palm on her knee.

Matty stood up and crept closer to the edge of the desk. When she reached her destination, she hunched forward and swatted at the mouse cord.

Watching how little it took to keep Matty happy cheered Kat somewhat. She took hold of the mouse again, shaking it for Matty's benefit. "First, I'm going to look up those public records you mentioned."

"Okay."

Kat worked in silence for a long time. The only sounds in the room came from the keyboard clacking and Tom and Matty purring.

Tom didn't even seem to care that Kat had stopped petting him. He seemed perfectly content just to be snuggled up next to his human. Meanwhile, the weight of the feline's body in her lap kept Kat calm and focused.

But an hour later, Kat felt more frustrated than ever.

"My search of Washington State records turned up nothing." Kat frowned at her computer monitor. "It's like she vanished into thin air."

"Or she just doesn't have much of an online presence," Andrew said, obviously trying to buoy her hopes.

She sagged against her chair. "What do we do if she's not online?"

"Simple," Andrew said. "We'll track down anybody who lived in town in the eighties and talk to them."

CHAPTER THREE

The next morning Kat arrived for her waitressing shift at Jessie's Diner right on time. As usual, the charming scents of whatever Jessie Polanski had on special tickled her nostrils as soon as she stepped through the front door.

Jessie was tallying something at the cash register, but she looked up when Kat walked in. "Morning, Kat."

"Hi, Jessie." Kat tossed her purse under the counter and breathed in deeply. "It smells delicious in here."

Jessie fingered a lock of brown hair that had escaped her bun and hooked it behind her ear. "I'm cooking up a new soup. Carrot ginger."

Kat grabbed a clean apron and slipped it over her head. "Based on the way my mouth is watering, it's going to be a hit."

"I hope so."

Kat picked up a sleeve of napkins and started refilling the dispensers on the counter. The mindless work allowed her thoughts to drift to Andrew's words from the night before and his suggestion to question anyone who might possibly have information on Maybelle Harper.

Kat peeked over at her boss, who was tapping on a calculator. Although Jessie had been fairly young herself when Kat was a child, she was still eight years older—old enough for her memories of the mid-eighties to be more solid than Kat's. And her family had owned the most popular restaurant in town, a place where the locals often gathered to gossip. There was a chance she might remember hearing something concerning where Kat's mother had moved to.

Plus, Kat had a lot of respect for Jessie. She had taken over managing the diner from her parents sometime during Kat's fifteen-year absence from Cherry Hills, and, rather than running the business into the ground, the already successful restaurant had only flourished even more.

Kat set the package of napkins on the counter and took a deep breath. "Jessie, can I ask you something?"

"Sure." She twisted around and propped her hip against the counter. "What's up?"

"I've decided to look for my mother."

Jessie's eyes widened, but she didn't say anything.

Kat folded her hands in front of her, feeling awkward. "I haven't been able to find any information on the Internet, and Andrew suggested I ask everybody whether they know where she could be, so . . ."

"So you figured you might as well hit me up for info," Jessie filled in.

Kat nodded.

"Well, I hate to disappoint you, but I don't remember her."

Kat had figured as much, but she still couldn't prevent the dejection that sank in when she heard the words spoken aloud.

"Mom should though," Jessie went on.

Kat straightened. "You think so?"

"Sure. She knew most everybody in town. I don't know if she'd know your mom's present whereabouts, but I could call her up if you want."

"I'd really appreciate that."

"Or, you can drive over to Spokane and visit her in person." Jessie grinned. "She always liked you."

"Mrs. Polanski was good to me," Kat said, smiling at the old memories. "She never failed to give me milkshakes on the house."

Jessie laughed. "That wasn't something she did for all the neighborhood kids, you know. She only gave free milkshakes to you—and Andrew when he came in with you."

Kat didn't know what to say to that. She hadn't realized she'd received special treatment, and the knowledge caused a dull ache to sprout in the center of her chest. She should have shown more appreciation for Mrs. Polanski's kindness back then.

Jessie reached into a basket next to the register and pulled out an order pad and pen. She jotted something down, then tore off the top sheet. "Here's Mom's address and phone number. She'd love to hear from you."

Kat took the page and slipped it into her pants pocket. "Thanks. Maybe I will go visit her."

Jessie tapped the pen against her chin. "You know, if you don't want to make the trip over to Spokane you could talk to my aunt. Helen Trotter. Did you ever meet her?"

Kat tried to place the name but came up blank. "I don't think so."

"She knew pretty much everybody in town,

same as Mom. And she still lives in Cherry Hills."

"I'd love to talk to her, if she's willing."

Jessie grinned. "Trust me, Aunt Helen's always up for a chat. Just be prepared to spend the whole day listening to boring old stories. She isn't above holding people prisoner in her house, and she'll babble on until your ears are sore."

If those stories concerned her mother, Kat was more than willing to suffer from a sore ear for a couple days. "Could you give me her number?"

"Sure." Jessie wrote something on another order sheet and handed it to Kat. "I'll call her up later and tell her to expect you."

"Great. Thanks so much, Jessie."

"Oh, you're the one doing Aunt Helen the favor. She's what you would call your proverbial cat lady." A shadow crossed over Jessie's face. "Ever since Uncle Nick died, she's been so lonely. I always hoped she'd find somebody else, but I guess that wasn't in the cards."

"I'm sorry. How long ago did your uncle pass on?"

"Eh, maybe twenty years now." Jessie sighed. "It wasn't a shock really. He was always in and out of hospitals."

"That's so sad."

Jessie shrugged. "Hey, that's life, right?"

"I guess so."

Jessie offered her a wry smile. "Some people lose their husbands, and some lose their mothers."

Kat's chest tightened. "Unfortunately."

Jessie snapped her fingers. "I should call up Mom and tell her to drive over for the day. Then the three of you can all sit down together."

"Really?" The thought of seeing Mrs. Polanski again cheered her. "You think she'd come?"

"For you, definitely. She's been talking about paying a visit to Aunt Helen for a while anyway. This will just speed her along."

Before they could say anything more, Kat felt her cell phone buzz in her pants pocket. She pulled it out, her heart skipping a beat when she spotted Andrew's name.

She glanced at Jessie. "Do you mind if I take this?"

Jessie turned back to the register. "Go right ahead."

Kat walked a few steps away and connected the call. "Hi."

"Where are you?" Andrew asked without preamble.

"Jessie's."

"You're working?"

"Yes."

"Stop by the police station when you get off."

Kat gripped the phone harder, not missing the urgency in his voice. "What is it? What's wrong?"

"Nothing that can't wait until your shift is over," he said.

"You won't tell me now?"

"I don't have any details to tell, but I found somebody who has information about your mother."

Kat's breath caught. "What kind of information?"

"I don't know. You'll have to come by the station and hear it yourself."

Kat frowned. "You won't tell me anything now?"

"I don't know anything. Chief says he'd rather talk to you directly."

"Chief?" Kat repeated. "You mean your police chief?"

"Yes. He's been with the force since the eighties, when your mom still lived here."

Kat's stomach lurched. She didn't have to ask why a police officer from thirty years ago would remember her mother. It wasn't a secret that she had been a drug addict, and Kat would be foolish not to consider that she might have a record.

She took a deep breath, reminding herself that she didn't have the luxury of only seeking out people who might recall Maybelle Harper in a positive light.

"You still there?" Andrew said.

Kat snapped to attention. "I'm here."

"So, I'll see you later, okay?"

"Okay. Bye."

Kat hung up and slumped against the counter, itching to find out what the police chief would reveal. But as eager as she was to race out of the restaurant and head straight for the police station, she couldn't do that to Jessie.

Until her shift ended, she would just have to tamp down her burning curiosity and try to concentrate on work as best she could.

CHAPTER FOUR

Kat drove as fast as she dared to Cherry Hills Police Department headquarters after her shift ended at three. The officer at the front desk eyed her warily as she barged into the building.

"Can I help you?" he asked.

"I'm Kat Harper," she told him. "I'm here to see—"

"Andrew, right." The officer grinned. "We've heard all about the new love of his life."

Kat blushed, unsure how to respond to that.

The officer rose from his chair and gestured for her to follow him. "He's in his office."

Andrew stood up when they arrived. "You made it," he said to Kat.

The officer smirked before slinking away.

Andrew walked around to the other side of his desk and grasped Kat's elbow. "Come on."

She let him lead her back into the hallway. "Where are we going?"

"Chief's office."

Andrew headed toward a room at the end of the hallway. Unlike his own office, this one actually had windows, both on the inside and outside walls. The blinds were open, allowing Kat to see straight through to the lawn spread out behind the station.

She shifted her focus to the huge man sitting behind the desk, guessing he was the police chief. He looked as if he could bench-press the building without breaking a sweat.

As though he'd sensed her scrutiny, he lifted his head and motioned for them to enter before Andrew could knock.

"Chief, this is Kat Harper," Andrew said, releasing her elbow. "Kat, meet Chief Kenny."

"Kat!" the police chief boomed, hefting his sizable frame from a chair constructed for someone significantly smaller. He held out a forearm the thickness of a tree trunk.

Kat shook his hand. "It's nice to meet you."

"We met when you were a tot, but I doubt you'd remember that." The chief's handshake almost dislocated her shoulder. Thankfully, he let go after two pumps. "You weren't much bigger than a grain of rice back then."

Kat rubbed her palm, surreptitiously checking for broken bones. "No, sorry. I don't remember."

Chief Kenny heaved himself back into his seat. "No worries."

Andrew sat down in one of the visitor chairs. "So, Chief, what do you know about Maybelle Harper that you wouldn't tell me until Kat arrived?"

Kat held her breath as she perched in the chair next to Andrew.

Chief Kenny folded his arms on the desk and looked at her. "I was a beat cop back when Maybelle lived here, before she disappeared."

"Disappeared?" The word sent a small shiver racing down Kat's spine. "From Cherry Hills, you mean."

Chief Kenny nodded. "Yep, from Cherry Hills, but also in general. Wherever she ended up, she hasn't left behind a paper trail."

Kat stared at him, trying to ward off the sinking sensation threatening to engulf her entire being. "You mean she's just . . . gone?" She'd never imagined her mother had dropped off the face of the earth when she'd failed to uncover information on her the night before.

She just figured she hadn't used the most effective search terms or accessed the right public records database.

Chief Kenny flapped his hand. "Gone, hightailed it out of town, on the lam, whatever you wanna call it."

"On the lam?" Kat repeated, her tongue tripping over the words. "You mean she's wanted?"

"Yep. You didn't know?"

Kat shook her head, feeling numb. "I just figured she moved away and didn't keep in touch with anybody."

"It was more complicated than that." Chief Kenny folded his giant hands behind his head and leaned back in his chair. "It was a big deal 'round here when she disappeared, but you woulda been too young to remember." He squinted at her. "Still, I figured you woulda heard something 'bout it by now. Small town like this, word travels fast."

"Nobody ever talked to me about her." To be fair, Kat had never asked. When she was younger the topic of her mother had seemed sacred. Back then, discussing her real mother with those acting as temporary substitutes had felt like the ultimate betrayal.

Chief Kenny dropped his hands back onto the desk and looked Kat straight in the eye.

"You know 'bout that bank robbery that happened 'round here in '85?"

"No."

"That doesn't surprise me." He grinned. "News had died down a little by the time you could talk. You ever heard of PNW Financial?"

Kat shook her head, an eerie sensation washing over her. She wasn't sure what Chief Kenny was getting at, but she had a bad feeling about it.

"It was a bank that operated 'round these parts here," he explained. "They were taken over back in the nineties, then again 'bout ten years later. I believe they're part of Wells Fargo now."

"Okay," Kat said slowly.

Chief Kenny settled back in his seat. "The gist of it is that one of the Wenatchee branches was robbed 'round the time Maybelle disappeared. The thief made off with about ten grand."

Kat's jaw dropped open. "And they weren't caught?"

"Nope. A photo of the robber taken from the security footage landed on our desk here. Folks on the Wenatchee force asked everybody in a hundred-mile radius to be on the lookout for the woman."

Kat swallowed. “The robber was a woman?”

“Yep.”

She didn’t reply. She had a distinct sense where he was headed, and she didn’t like it.

Chief Kenny pursed his lips. “Cameras weren’t like they are now, you understand, but the short of it is that your mama’s wanted.”

“For bank robbery,” Kat said, feeling numb.

Chief Kenny aimed a beefy finger at her. “Exactamundo.”

“You’re not sure she did it though, right?” Andrew interjected.

Kat glanced at him. He looked as surprised as she felt.

“We ain’t positive, but the case has never been solved and she disappeared that same week,” Chief Kenny said. “Wenatchee tried to trace the bills taken, but that was a dead end.”

Kat straightened, clinging to the sliver of hope he’d planted. “So she could be innocent.”

Chief Kenny lifted his massive shoulders. “Could be. Hard to say since we weren’t ever able to talk to her. She just up and left.”

“Maybe she left for another reason,” Kat proposed.

“Like I said, could be. It sure woulda been nice if we coulda heard her side of the story though.”

Kat didn't say anything. She really had no good explanation for why anyone would run away right after a big bank robbery if they weren't somehow involved.

But she wasn't about to admit this to a police chief and implicate her own mother.

Chief Kenny coughed. "Kat, I hate to say this, but your mama didn't exactly have the best habits."

Although she figured everyone who had lived in Cherry Hills thirty years ago knew about her mother's drug addiction, his words still made her internal organs feel as if they were being compressed in a vise.

"I won't tell you everything she was into, but it was some pretty bad stuff," he continued. "Stuff that rots the brain and ain't likely to make even the most levelheaded individual act rationally. And some of that stuff could cost a person a good chunk of dough."

Kat folded her hands over her stomach. "You think she robbed that bank for drug money."

Chief Kenny held up his hands. "What I think doesn't really matter. I only want you to be aware of the facts here."

"I know she wasn't a model citizen," Kat conceded. "But I'd still like to find her."

He nodded. “I understand. Unfortunately, I can’t help you there.”

“Well, thank you for telling me all this anyway.” Although she had been hoping for a better lead, she still appreciated the information.

Chief Kenny snapped forward in his chair, his elbows landing on the desk. “Now it’s my turn to ask you for a favor.”

Kat stilled. “What’s that?”

His eyes bored into hers. “When you find your mama, tell her I’m still waiting to speak with her.”

CHAPTER FIVE

"Maybe this isn't such a good idea," Kat said as Andrew escorted her out of the station.

He darted her a glance. "What do you mean?"

Kat kicked a stone out of their path. "I mean, what if my mother did rob that bank?" Asking the question out loud aggravated the sick feeling in the pit of her stomach. "If I find her, I could be getting her into trouble."

The thought had been gnawing on Kat since they'd stepped foot out of Chief Kenny's office. As enthusiastic as she had been earlier to talk to the police chief, now she had to wonder if she might be doing more harm than good.

Andrew took her hand in his. "That's certainly a possibility you have to keep in mind."

Kat halted as a thought seized her. "What's the statute of limitations on bank robbery?"

Andrew stopped beside her. "I'd have to check. But you do realize the statute of limitations is put on hold when a person becomes a fugitive from the law, right? In your mother's case, if she reappeared it would be like the past thirty years never happened."

"Oh." Kat felt her shoulders slip a little lower.

They resumed their trek across the parking lot in silence. She wondered if she would be better off looking for her mother without Andrew's help. Although she didn't want to start off their relationship keeping secrets, she might not have a choice. As an officer of the law, he might have a moral obligation to notify his superiors of anything she told him concerning her runaway mother.

Andrew cleared his throat. "I guess the question you have to ask yourself is whether you'd be able to live without knowing if you opted to drop this whole thing."

"I've lived thirty-two years without knowing," she said. "Another thirty-two should be a cinch."

But despite the lightness she forced into her

tone, her heart wasn't in the words. She'd already lived thirty-two years too long in the dark. She didn't think she could go her whole lifetime without at least trying to get at the truth. Now that she'd given her mind permission to wonder, she couldn't shut it off so easily.

Kat tried to muster up a smile when they reached her car. "Thanks for talking to your chief on my behalf."

Andrew stared into her eyes, sending a tiny shiver through her body. "Kat, you know whatever you decide, I'm behind you."

She nodded. "I appreciate that."

He took both of her hands in his and grinned. "I really want to kiss you, but I'm not sure how you feel about having an audience."

Kat's eyes darted around. "We're the only people out here."

Andrew jerked his head toward the station. "Trust me, at least one of the guys is watching."

Although he meant it as a playful comment, the idea unnerved her. She extracted her hands from his and wrapped her arms around her body. The thought of someone spying on her when she felt so vulnerable had her yearning to put up some type of physical boundary.

Andrew shoved his hands in his pants pockets. "I'll catch up with you later then, okay?"

"Okay." She smiled at him. "We'll do the kiss then."

His eyes sparkled. "You're on."

Kat watched him walk back across the parking lot, her heart soaring. Every time she remembered their first kiss anew—an experience she thought about often—she felt almost giddy.

She truly hoped this business with her mother didn't change any of that.

Sighing, Kat fished her keys out of her purse and unlocked her car. Her phone rang as she was buckling her seat belt. She pulled it out of her pants pocket, Jessie's Diner popping up on the caller ID.

"Hello?" she answered.

"Hi, Kat. It's Jessie. I talked to Mom. She's going to drive over to Aunt Helen's tomorrow morning, if you want to stop by to ask about your mother."

Kat's pulse quickened. "Okay, great."

"Let me give you the address."

Kat rummaged through her purse for a pen and paper. "I'm ready."

Jessie relayed her aunt's address. "Just stop by anytime before your shift starts. Knowing Mom, she'll leave Spokane at the crack of dawn and stay until the sun sets." She laughed. "She couldn't leave earlier if she wanted to. They both love to talk."

"I'll be there. Thanks so much."

Kat slipped her phone back into her pocket, vowing to stop by Helen's house first thing in the morning.

She only hoped she didn't learn anything that put her in the position of hiding information from the police—or Andrew.

CHAPTER SIX

Helen Trotter lived on the outskirts of town. As Kat parked and headed up the driveway toward the tiny, blue house the next morning, she wondered if Helen and Mrs. Polanski believed her mother to be as guilty of the 1985 bank robbery as Chief Kenny did. The thought of Maybelle Harper having already been tried and convicted by the court of public opinion made her uneasy.

Still, she was loath to ignore a potential lead.

Kat stepped onto the porch. Two yellow eyes framed by a furry, black-and-white face followed her movements. When the cat realized she'd spotted him, he flicked his tail.

Kat crouched down and extended her fingers toward him. “Hi, kitty.”

The cat peered curiously at her outstretched hand, but after a moment he turned his head and gazed into the yard. Kat figured he’d been disappointed by the lack of treats in her palm.

Appropriately dismissed, Kat stood back up and rang the doorbell, glancing around as she waited. Helen’s house was rather rundown, with paint peeling off of the exterior and a few loose shingles hanging from the roof. Even so, it didn’t look any worse than the other homes in the neighborhood.

A cloud floated in front of the morning sun, casting a shadow over the spot where Kat was standing. She wrapped her arms around herself, hoping nature wasn’t trying to forebode how her visit today would end.

The front door creaked open. Before Kat had time to redirect her attention, she felt two pudgy arms snaking around her shoulders.

“Glory be, if it isn’t Kat Harper come back to see me!” a familiar voice from Kat’s childhood said, crushing her against her soft chest.

Kat grinned as she pulled away. “It’s good to see you too, Mrs. Polanski. You haven’t changed a bit.” The woman who used to run Jessie’s Diner still wore her brown hair cut in the same no-nonsense bob, could light up a room with her smile, and carried enough extra weight around her middle that hugging her felt like embracing a favorite stuffed animal.

"Well, come in, come in." Mrs. Polanski grabbed Kat's arm and dragged her inside. "When Jess called to tell me you wanted to see me, I let out a whoop that could be heard all the way to Idaho."

Kat laughed. She had forgotten how feisty Mrs. Polanski was, and she was glad the woman hadn't lost any of her energy since they'd seen each other last.

Mrs. Polanski hauled Kat into a small sitting room, where another woman was already seated. "Helen, this here is one of the finest kids you'll ever meet."

"Kat Harper," the woman said, nodding. "Nora's told me all about you. It's a pleasure to meet you in person."

"Nice to meet you, too." Kat searched for a resemblance between the sisters but couldn't pick up any likeness besides their bright, brown eyes. Whereas Mrs. Polanski was on the heavy side and didn't appear to have aged at all in the past fifteen years, Helen had a more slender build and hadn't bothered to hide the gray hair and facial wrinkles suggestive of a woman over sixty.

Kat's eyes alighted on a framed photograph on one of the end tables. In it, thirty-something versions of the two sisters smiled for the camera, their arms swung around each other's waists. Mrs. Polanski was thinner in the photo but otherwise unchanged. The taller brunette with her hair cut to her shoulders had to be Helen. Even back then they didn't look so similar.

Her gaze strayed, a glance around the rest of the living room confirming what Jessie had meant when she'd called her aunt a cat lady. Kat counted seven felines of various sizes and colors before Mrs. Polanski diverted her attention again.

"Tell us what's been going on with you," she said, a hungry expression on her face. She nudged aside a couple tabbies before plunking onto the couch, dragging Kat down beside her.

Kat twisted her hands in her lap, remembering her reason for being here. But before she could say anything, Mrs. Polanski started talking again.

"How long has it been since we saw each other?"

"Fifteen years."

"Fifteen years!" Mrs. Polanski shook her head. "What have you been doing all that time?"

"School and work, mostly. I just moved back to Cherry Hills a couple months ago. Did Jessie tell you I'm waitressing at the diner?"

"Of course! Jess says you're a model employee."

Kat shifted positions. "Oh, well."

One of the tabbies that had lost his seat jumped on Kat's lap. He gave her an appraising look as he kneaded her thighs. Apparently she passed whatever test he'd subjected her to because he settled down and started to purr.

"But Jess said that was only a temporary thing for you," Mrs. Polanski went on.

Kat nodded, running her hand down the tabby's back. "I'd really like to get a job in computer programming."

Mrs. Polanski beamed as if Kat had announced she'd discovered a cure for cancer. "I always knew you were a smart one. Didn't I tell you, Helen? Didn't I tell you this one was going places?"

"You sure did," Helen said.

"And now look at her." Mrs. Polanski peered at Kat with undisguised admiration. "She's fixing to get herself a fancy-pants high-tech job."

Kat's cheeks flushed. "Oh, well. I haven't actually found any positions in my field yet."

Mrs. Polanski slapped her palms on her

thighs. "Why, I bet one day you'll be on TV telling everybody about the robot you invented to perform surgery or fly jets. Are you working on anything like that?"

"Uh, no."

"Well, you will," Mrs. Polanski said, patting Kat's hand. "Once them geniuses in Silicon Valley find out you exist, they're going to try to steal you away from Cherry Hills. Mark my words."

Kat focused on thoroughly scratching the tabby's chin so she wouldn't have to look directly at Mrs. Polanski. She wasn't used to receiving so much praise.

"Jessie tells me you're looking for your mama," Mrs. Polanski barreled on.

Kat snapped her head up, startled by the abrupt subject change. "Yes, actually, I am."

"I might be able to help you out there." Mrs. Polanski stood up and bustled over to a kitchen table barely big enough to seat two. She brushed a few cats aside and picked up a file folder, waving it around. "I brought some newspaper clippings I saved from the eighties."

Kat sat up a little straighter. "Is my mother mentioned in any of them?"

Mrs. Polanski ambled back over to the sofa and held the folder out to Kat. "Well, now, you'll have to go through them and see for yourself."

Kat held her breath as she took the folder, her heart soaring with hope. If something in here led her to Maybelle Harper she would be eternally grateful.

Careful not to disturb the tabby, she set the folder on the empty couch cushion next to her and flipped the top open. The newspaper clippings inside were yellowed with age but still in good shape. She studied the top one, a half-page article dated June 28, 1985. It was a review of a restaurant called Country Eats that had opened that winter down in Estacada, Oregon.

Mrs. Polanski reseated herself. "Every now and then something in the news catches my attention. What you're holding there are some of the things that captured my fancy around the time your mama left town."

Kat riffled through the pages. The folder included everything from opinion pieces on the best places to live in the Pacific Northwest to obituaries of people who had died thirty years ago.

"I miss the days when every place had a paper," Mrs. Polanski said. "The *Cherry Hills Courant* was my favorite, though I read the big publications from Seattle and Spokane too." She smiled. "Maybe my collection will help you on your quest."

Kat closed the folder, pushing aside her disappointment. Unless she wanted to know where to find the best prime rib dinner in rural Oregon, she wasn't sure how these articles would help. Still, she appreciated Mrs. Polanski's willingness to assist. "Thank you."

Kat darted a look at Helen, who had taken out what looked to be a half-finished scarf patterned in Christmas colors. The knitting needles in her hands clicked together at a steady pace. She seemed oblivious to the two cats batting at the yarn as it unraveled.

Kat turned back to Mrs. Polanski. "Maybe you could tell me a little bit about my mother. Did you know her?"

Mrs. Polanski brightened. "Oh, yes. Maybelle was a sweet woman. Had a smile that could make a man fall instantly in love and a laugh warm enough to melt steel."

An ache blossomed in Kat's chest. She wished she remembered that.

"Of course, she had her own share of problems," Mrs. Polanski continued. "She didn't always hang with the best crowds or make good decisions, mind you, but she had a heart of pure gold."

Kat swallowed hard. "You're referring to the

bank she's accused of holding up?"

The whole room seemed to freeze. Mrs. Polanski's wide eyes stared unblinkingly, and Helen's knitting needles came to a standstill. The two cats swatting at the yarn dropped their paws to the floor and stood like statues. Even the tabby in Kat's lap stopped purring.

Mrs. Polanski was the first to move. She reached down and picked up an all-black cat resting underneath the coffee table. She set him in her lap and scratched his ears for a moment before saying, "Actually, I was referring to Maybelle's drug addiction."

Kat frowned. "Oh. I guess I have the robbery on my brain, since I just learned about it."

Mrs. Polanski patted Kat's elbow. "You were too young to remember. By the time you got to the point where you were toddling about town on your own, there were bigger and better things to talk about."

"The stock market crash," Helen piped up.

"Oh, yes, Black Monday." Mrs. Polanski shook her head. "Didn't really affect Helen and me. We weren't into stocks. But you should have heard some of the other folks in town discussing how much money they lost."

"When was this?"

"A couple years later," Mrs. Polanski said.

"October '87."

Kat's brain churned. Assuming her mother wasn't guilty, she couldn't help but wonder if the person who had robbed that bank might have invested their loot only to lose it all two years later.

"Who was affected by the crash?" she asked.

"Oh, anybody with investments." Mrs. Polanski grinned ruefully. "Even I lost a bit, although we really only dabbled in the market."

"What about single women?" Kat said, shifting as the tabby began grooming himself. "Were any of them hit hard?"

Mrs. Polanski's forehead furrowed. "Single women?"

Kat bit her lip, debating whether to let the two sisters in on her speculations. She didn't figure she had much to lose. "Chief Kenny, the CHPD police chief, says the bank's security cameras caught a woman on tape. I was thinking if my mother didn't rob that bank, it was likely another single woman. I mean, a woman wouldn't rob a bank alone if she were married, would she? Wouldn't her husband have done it? You'd think he would be more menacing, and therefore less likely to encounter resistance."

Mrs. Polanski's mouth had gaped open sometime during Kat's speech. She clamped it shut, then said, “Well, that’s quite a theory.”

Kat’s spirits sank. “You think my mother did it.”

“Oh, I didn’t say that.”

But from the way Mrs. Polanski darted a look at Helen, she didn’t have to say it. Kat could tell she thought her mother was guilty.

Kat looked down at her lap, feeling a pinch of shame. She watched with envy as the tabby stuck one hind leg straight up in the air so he could clean it, wishing she could be as blissfully content as the cat. Although rationally she knew she shouldn’t feel responsible for anything her mother might have done, she couldn’t convince her heart. As the only Harper left in the area—as far as she knew—she was the only person around to absorb the blame for any crimes committed by her kin.

“Helen,” Mrs. Polanski said, squinting at the cat in her lap, “this little fella looks like he’s under the weather.”

Helen set down her knitting, a troubled look crossing over her face. “That’s Shadow. I told you he hasn’t been feeling well, remember?”

“Oh, yes.” Mrs. Polanski fingered the animal’s ribs. “Is he eating properly? He feels thin.”

Helen shook her head. “He nibbles here and

there, but his appetite isn't what it used to be."

"You ought to take him to the vet."

Helen wrung her hands together. "I can't afford that."

Kat looked at Shadow, who wasn't reacting much to Mrs. Polanski's poking and prodding. "I volunteer for 4F."

Helen tilted her head. "4F?"

"Furry Friends Foster Families," Kat clarified. "It's a nonprofit. We could help cover his vet bills."

Helen's face brightened. "Really?"

Kat nodded. "In fact, I can get him checked out after I leave here, if you'd like."

Helen rubbed her palms together. "Oh, that would be fantastic. I hate for him to suffer any longer than necessary."

Kat glanced at the clock. "I should probably head out now. I have to be at Jessie's by three."

"Grab a carrier from the coat closet," Helen said, gesturing.

"Okay." Kat lifted the tabby off her lap, prompting the feline to give her a questioning look. But when she set him down again, he went back to his bath as if he'd never been interrupted.

Kat fetched a top-opening carrier from the closet. She placed it on the floor and held the hatch open while Mrs. Polanski lowered Shadow inside. Shadow didn't protest, not even when Kat shut the hatch.

Kat picked up the carrier. "I'll return him as soon as the vet says he's good to go," she assured Helen.

The worry lines framing Helen's mouth deepened. "I'd appreciate that."

Mrs. Polanski grabbed the file folder. "Don't forget this. Something in here could help you."

Although Kat doubted that, she didn't say anything as she followed Mrs. Polanski to the front door.

Mrs. Polanski had to sweep a few cats out of the way before stepping outside. She patted Kat's shoulder as they walked. "Your mama, she was a kind woman. I don't want you thinking ill of her."

Kat looked down at the driveway. She didn't really know what to think. When she'd first let herself imagine what a reunion would be like, she'd pictured her and Maybelle hugging and laughing and crying over all the lost years, both of them overjoyed to have found each other again. Even in her darker fantasies Maybelle would merely tell Kat to get lost and hang up the phone, leaving both of them free to go on with their separate lives.

Now, she had to account for the possibility that if she did find her mother, Chief Kenny might be waiting on the sidelines with a pair of handcuffs.

"There are lots of reasons why somebody might find themselves in the type of situation where they needed to take money that wasn't theirs," Mrs. Polanski continued. "Some aren't as terrible as they might seem."

Kat glanced at her. "What are you saying? You think my mother robbed that bank for honorable reasons?"

Mrs. Polanski frowned. "I'm saying, don't jump to conclusions. Nobody ever got anywhere good from making hasty assumptions."

A weight settled in Kat's chest as she busied herself with strapping Shadow's carrier in the back seat. As futile as she knew it was to speculate, she couldn't shut off her brain so easily.

When Kat emerged from the car, Mrs. Polanski pulled her in for another hug. "It was good seeing you. I do miss you, you know."

Kat returned the hug briefly before taking a step back. "I've missed you too."

Mrs. Polanski handed Kat the folder. "Next time, don't wait so long between visits."

"Okay," Kat replied, even though she knew Mrs. Polanski was just being polite.

Still, the thought of never seeing another adult from her childhood was too sad to consider at the moment, even if that adult didn't hold her mother in the best light.

CHAPTER SEVEN

During the drive to the vet's office, Kat couldn't stop thinking about her visit with Helen and Mrs. Polanski. She kept turning back to the point in their conversation when Mrs. Polanski had talked about the stock market crash, unable to shake the notion that someone else had robbed that bank in the hopes of getting rich quick, first by taking money that wasn't theirs, then by investing in an attempt to build an even bigger fortune.

Kat sighed, silently acknowledging that her scenario might be a little far-fetched. After all, would someone commit a felony only to buy stocks? A bank robbery was more likely to be executed by someone who needed money, not someone who merely wanted more. Was she only brainstorming wild motives to better convince herself of her mother's innocence?

Shadow's carrier shifted in the back seat, wrenching Kat's thoughts back to the present. She stopped for a red light and twisted around, spying the cat's dull, yellow eyes focused on her through the slats of his cage.

"Hang in there," Kat told him. "We're going to get you all better, and then return you to Helen."

Shadow didn't say anything. Kat hoped that meant he was content with this plan.

The light turned green, and Kat continued up the street until she reached Cherry Hills Veterinary. She parked, extricated Shadow's carrier with as little jostling as possible, and entered the office.

Imogene Little was standing at the reception counter when Kat walked in. "Kat!" she greeted, waving so vigorously that her auburn ponytail danced.

Kat smiled at her fellow Furry Friends Foster Families volunteer. "Hi, Imogene."

"What are you doing here?"

"I was visiting with Helen Trotter, Jessie Polanski's aunt, and she mentioned one of her cats hasn't been feeling well." Kat lifted up Shadow's carrier. "She said she didn't have any money for vet care so I offered 4F's assistance."

"Oh, good. I hate to see an animal suffer because of financial reasons."

Kat set the carrier on one of the plastic lobby chairs. "What about you? What brings you here today?"

Imogene poked her finger between the carrier slats to scratch the bridge of Shadow's nose, prompting the feline to close his eyes and begin purring. "One of our foster cats is getting some stitches removed."

"Anything serious?"

"No, just a few injuries from a fight he got into before we rescued him. He's all better now." Imogene reached into her jeans pocket and pulled out a folded sheet of paper. "In fact, since you're here I'll give you the invoice now."

Kat took it from her and slipped it into her own pants pocket. "I'll add it to what 4F owes when I process the bills this weekend."

Imogene smiled. "I know you'll take care of it."

Kat walked toward the redheaded receptionist. "Hi, Sherry. I have a sick cat I'd like Dr. Harry to look at on behalf of 4F."

"Good to see you again, Katherine." Sherry tapped on her keyboard. "I'll fit you right in."

"Thanks."

Imogene straightened as Kat rejoined her. "I heard you've been asking around about your mother."

Kat stilled. Sometimes she forgot how quickly word traveled in a town like Cherry Hills, and how news seemed to reach Imogene in particular at the speed of light.

"I heard it from somebody at the police station," Imogene went on, as if reading Kat's mind. "They said Andrew's been making inquiries on your behalf. Is that true?"

Kat nodded. "I talked to Chief Kenny yesterday."

"What did he have to say?"

"That my mother disappeared right after PNW Financial was held up in 1985." Saying the words out loud resurrected the nausea Kat felt whenever she let herself consider that her mother might have committed such a crime.

Imogene adjusted her ponytail. "I remember that. Happened in Wenatchee, and most people believed Maybelle was guilty, including the police."

"She hasn't been positively linked to the robbery," Kat said, hearing the note of defensiveness in her tone. "Chief Kenny says he only wants to question her."

"I didn't mean to imply anything otherwise,"

Imogene assured her. "But you do have to admit the timing is rather strange."

Kat didn't say anything, mainly because she couldn't disagree.

Imogene scrutinized her. "You don't believe she's guilty?"

Kat folded her arms across her chest. "I'm not really sure what to believe."

Imogene patted Kat's elbow. "Naturally. A girl always feels ties to her mother, no matter how estranged they might be. Without knowing your roots, it's hard to find your place in the world."

Kat rocked backward, her hands dropping to her sides. She was surprised Imogene had pegged her so accurately. It made her realize she really didn't know all that much about her fellow Furry Friends Foster Families board member.

Imogene glanced at Shadow. "I didn't really socialize with Maybelle, you know, but I heard things."

Kat's stomach clenched. From Imogene's tone, she gathered anything she'd heard had been negative. Still, she was desperate.

"What can you tell me about her?" Kat asked, fortifying herself.

"That she was troubled, for one thing."

Imogene paused, as if conflicted over what she had to say next.

"I know she used drugs," Kat volunteered, hoping to encourage her friend to open up.

Imogene's lips puckered. "That's true, but that's a rather simple way of putting it."

"What do you mean?"

"Your mom, she wanted something better for herself. I think she just struggled to find out how to achieve it."

Kat absorbed that, trying to reconcile Imogene's observation with a woman on the run after robbing a bank.

Imogene lowered herself into one of the waiting room chairs. "You know, the rumors about her motive for that bank robbery never really made sense to me."

Kat sat down on the other side of Shadow's carrier. "They didn't?"

Imogene shook her head. "People liked to say Maybelle had hit rock bottom, but I didn't believe it. It just seemed so out of character, Maybelle doing something like that. Your mom, she was trying to shake her drug habit. It didn't make sense that she would regress so severely all of a sudden."

"If you don't think my mother robbed that bank, why do you think she disappeared at the same time?"

Imogene held her palms up. "I can't say she didn't hold up that bank, I can only tell you my perception of Maybelle the last few times I saw her."

"You don't have any theories?" Kat pressed. With Imogene having such a favorable impression of her mother, she was itching to hear her opinion.

Imogene bit her lip. "Naturally, I've thought about it over the years."

Kat leaned across Shadow's carrier. "I'd like to know what you concluded."

"Well, I never really came to any definite conclusions," Imogene hedged. "You have to remember, I didn't know Maybelle all that well."

Kat had to resist her urge to drop to one knee on the floor. "Please."

Imogene regarded her for a long moment. Finally, she nodded, seeming to register Kat's desperation. "I thought, perhaps, that she had robbed that bank for more noble reasons than others in town gave her credit for."

"Noble reasons?"

"Like to get her life in order." Imogene offered her a sad smile. "She loved you, you know. That I don't doubt for a second."

Kat stuck two fingers between the carrier

slats and absently stroked Shadow's back. She hadn't realized until then how much she needed to hear that her mother had cared about her, and Imogene's words caused tears to spring to her eyes.

Imogene crossed her legs. "But, naturally, she couldn't care for you while she was still battling her own demons."

"The drugs, you mean," Kat said.

"Yes. And getting help for that sort of thing isn't cheap."

Kat tried to wrap her brain around what Imogene was saying. "So you think my mother robbed that bank in order to pay for treatment?"

Imogene shrugged. "Like I said, this is all speculation on my part."

"But it makes sense." And, Kat had to admit, it was a much more palatable theory than the notion of her mother only committing a felony in order to further fund her drug habit.

"I *do* know that rehab is not inexpensive," Imogene continued. "A woman of Maybelle's means . . . well, she wasn't the type to have access to such resources under normal circumstances."

Kat bobbed her head, feeling herself warming to her friend's supposition. "Right."

"And I believe she was motivated to regain custody of you." Imogene sighed. "A mother who's had her child ripped from her arms might feel inclined to do some things she might not do otherwise, things she might typically find morally reprehensible. You understand?"

"Yes, that makes complete sense." Although, Kat had to wonder if she'd only embraced Imogene's theory because it supported her own yearning for her mother to have cared.

Their conversation was interrupted when Sherry called out, "Katherine Harper? Dr. Harry will meet you in Room B."

"Thanks." Kat gripped Shadow's carrier as she stood up. "Thank you, Imogene, for sharing what you know. You have no idea what it means to me."

Imogene reached out and patted Kat's hand. "I hope you find her. A girl shouldn't have to go through life wondering about her mother."

Kat firmed her hold on Shadow's carrier, the truth of Imogene's words weighing her down as she ducked into the hallway.

CHAPTER EIGHT

After leaving Cherry Hills Veterinary, Kat couldn't do much more than mope around her apartment. She kept dwelling on her conversation with Imogene. The thought of her mother needing to rob a bank in order to fund treatment for her drug addiction made her infinitely sad.

Of course, it was better than what Chief Kenny had hinted at, that her mother had only robbed a bank to support an ongoing addiction.

Kat had been sitting on her couch wallowing in her thoughts for a good twenty minutes when Matty finally joined her. The tortoiseshell licked Kat's hand before curling into a ball and burying her face in her front paws.

Kat smiled. She hoped Shadow was as comfortable as Matty appeared to be. Dr. Harry had told her the poor thing was extremely dehydrated thanks to a recent illness he was on the tail end of shaking. He had opted to keep the black cat on an IV overnight in order to get some fluids into his little body.

Kat's eyes strayed past Matty and landed on the file folder Mrs. Polanski had given her. Although she couldn't fathom how a bunch of old newspaper articles would help her find her mother, going through them would at least make her feel as if she were doing something productive.

Careful not to disturb Matty, Kat bent forward and pinched the folder between two fingers, pulling it toward her. She set it on her lap and flipped the cover open.

Her eyes alighted on the top article, a restaurant critic's write-up of Country Eats. She didn't expect to find anything useful, but she read through it anyway, looking for any references to her mother or PNW Financial. She even scrutinized the pictures of the various entrées, just in case a mysterious woman could be spotted in the background. There was nothing.

She set the article on the floor. Tom watched her from across the room, his ears pricking.

Soon afterward he ambled over, stepped gingerly onto the newsprint, and settled down as if he'd found a comfortable new bed.

Kat reached over and petted him. "If you see anything I missed, let me know."

Tom purred his agreement, although Kat gave up hope that he would be of any assistance when his eyes slipped shut.

She looked at the next clipping. This one was the obituaries page from the June 12, 1985 edition of the *Seattle Times*. Someone—Mrs. Polanski, she presumed—had circled the death notice of a pretty, twenty-seven-year-old woman named Kelly Watson. Kelly had died in a car accident, leaving behind her parents but no husband or children. None of the names mentioned were familiar to Kat, but maybe Kelly or one of her parents had been friends with Mrs. Polanski.

To be thorough, Kat read through the rest of the obituaries. Nothing stood out. Neither did she find anything of interest on the flip side of the page.

She leaned her head against the back of the couch, discouragement bubbling up inside her. Why Mrs. Polanski had thought a few random articles would advance her mission left her baffled.

Still, Kat didn't have any better leads.

The next clipping was a *Cherry Hills Courant* reporter's take on the PNW Financial robbery. Kat studied this one more closely, reading everything twice to make sure she didn't miss anything. But the article only went over a few cursory details. It made no mention of Maybelle being a suspect, and it didn't provide any information that Kat hadn't already learned from Chief Kenny.

Kat placed the article on the floor next to Tom, revealing an invoice from a Wenatchee hospital addressed to a Nick Trotter. The words 'second notice' were printed in red on top of the page. Kat figured the bill belonged to Helen's late husband and had gotten mixed up in Mrs. Polanski's things. She set it on the coffee table. She could return it to Helen when she brought Shadow back.

There were a couple more articles on the bank robbery interspersed with others concerning everything from the best places to live to apartments for rent. When Kat was three-quarters of the way through the folder she had long since given up poring over every word. Instead, she skimmed over each page and moved on if nothing struck her as relevant.

She was about to give up hope when she

spotted the words 'Maybelle Harper' embedded in one of the write-ups about the bank robbery. Her heart leapt into her throat, and she snatched up the page and read it as fast as she could. Although the reporter didn't outright accuse her mother of being guilty, the suggestion was pretty obvious from the way he described how she was 'wanted for questioning by local law enforcement agencies.'

Unfortunately, the article didn't tell her anything new.

Kat sighed. As though sensing her frustration, Matty stood up, set one of her paws on Kat's leg, and meowed.

Kat stroked her back. "I know, I know, I shouldn't lose hope."

Matty bobbed her head once as if to agree.

"But you have to admit this is pretty frustrating," Kat said, scratching between Matty's ears.

Matty meowed again before closing her eyes and pressing her head into Kat's hand.

Kat grinned. "I see some of Tom's chattiness is rubbing off on you. You usually don't meow unless you're hungry."

Matty meowed again as if to disagree.

Or, Kat thought, an eerie sensation washing over her, was Matty trying to tell her something about her mother?

Kat shook the thought away, feeling ridiculous. Was she getting so desperate for answers that she thought Matty had them?

When Matty meowed this time, she batted her paw at the folder in Kat's lap.

Kat frowned. "What is it, sweetheart?"

Matty jumped on the coffee table and sat down, her tail swishing.

Kat shivered as Matty's penetrating green eyes bored into her own. She knew Matty possessed an uncanny awareness of things, almost a sixth sense. Somehow she always knew when Kat needed a little extra love and would come over to give her hand a lick. And she never failed to predict when Kat had something unwelcome in mind, like a claw-trimming session. Kat had yet to figure out how Matty deduced what she was up to before she even took out the clippers.

Kat clutched her head in both hands, wondering if she was going crazy. After all, what could Matty possibly have to tell her about her mother?

And yet, no human had offered any answers so what did she really have to lose?

She refocused on the tortoiseshell. "What are you trying to tell me?"

Matty settled down on the coffee table, tucking her paws under her chest.

Kat glanced at where Matty had chosen to rest, as if the cat were deliberate about her napping spots and not prone to sleeping wherever she happened to be. Right now, Matty was lying on top of the Cherry Hills Veterinary invoice that Imogene had given her earlier.

Feeling a little foolish, Kat leaned forward and studied the invoice. The part that was visible above Matty itemized all the expenses Imogene had accrued during her visit. Peeking through Matty's fur at the bottom of the page was the total amount owed. Nothing struck Kat as peculiar. Certainly nothing revealed where her mother might be.

Kat flopped back against the couch, mentally chiding herself for actually believing Matty's actions were cloaked in hidden meaning.

Matty meowed again. When Kat looked up, she swore the feline shook her head in dismay.

"If you're trying to tell me something, you're going to have to be more blunt," Kat told her.

Matty flicked her tail in response. Then she began licking her paw, as though to indicate she'd done all she could.

Kat knew how she felt. If the past few days

was any indication of what she expected to learn during her search, she might simply have to come to terms with the possibility that she might never find her mother.

CHAPTER NINE

The next morning, Kat stopped by Cherry Hills Veterinary soon after they opened. Dr. Harry wasn't yet swamped with patients, and he motioned her back to one of the empty examination rooms.

"I'm happy to report that Shadow is doing much better now that we've got some fluids running through his system," he said.

Kat's relief sent the air rushing out of her lungs. "I'm glad."

"He should be fine, but if you notice anything amiss either bring him in again or give me a call."

"I'll let his owner know."

"Let me fetch him." Dr. Harry ducked out of the room and returned a minute later with a squirming cat carrier, which he set on the examination table. "Here you are."

Kat opened the hatch, eager to check on Shadow herself. Apparently, the black cat was just as eager to check out his surroundings. He poked his nose through the opening and peeked around the exam room. His eyes were much brighter, and from the way his head swiveled back and forth he looked to have regained some energy.

When Shadow braced his paws on the edge of the carrier as if to lift himself out, Kat gently closed the hatch. "Thank you so much, Dr. Harry."

"That's what I'm here for." He led her to the hallway. "Stop by Sherry's desk for your invoice."

"Okay."

Sherry had Shadow's bill in hand when Kat arrived at the reception desk. "The 4F rate has already been applied," the redhead chirped.

Kat gave the invoice a cursory glance as she took it. "Thanks. I'll add this to what Imogene owes you for her visit this week."

Sherry leaned back in her chair, smiling. "The charges sure do add up fast, don't they?"

"I'm just glad you all are so generous about discounting our bills." Kat adjusted her grip on

Shadow's carrier. "I'll send you a check when I balance the books this weekend."

Sherry waved her off. "No rush. We're always happy to help you guys out."

Kat headed for the door. "I appreciate it."

Outside, she unlocked her car, tossed the invoice on the passenger seat, and buckled Shadow's carrier into the back before starting off for Helen's house.

Shadow was much chattier on the return trip. Yesterday he'd spent the ride to the vet's hunkered down in indifferent silence. Today he meowed almost nonstop, a heartening sign of his improving health.

Evidently Helen was as anxious as Shadow for the cat to return home. She rushed out of the house before Kat had even shifted her car gear into park, as if she had been watching for their arrival all morning.

"How's Shadow?" Helen asked as soon as Kat opened her door.

Kat climbed out of the car. "He's fine."

The tension in Helen's shoulders evaporated. "Oh, thank goodness."

Kat extricated the carrier from the back seat. "He was dehydrated, but Dr. Harry kept him on an IV all night and he seems to have regained some energy."

Helen exhaled. "That's fantastic. You have no idea how much I appreciate this."

"I'm happy to help."

Shadow meowed, and Helen smiled. "He's telling us to set him free. He never did like that thing."

Kat followed Helen up the driveway. "I don't think any cat enjoys being confined."

Once Helen closed the front door, Kat set the carrier on the carpet and unlatched it. Several other cats wandered over to greet Shadow as he rejoined them. They touched noses in turn, and a few gave him welcoming head licks.

Kat stepped toward the door. "I have something else for you. Hang on." She ducked outside and returned seconds later with the hospital invoice she'd uncovered the day before.

Helen took it from her. "What's this?"

"It got mixed up in Mrs. Polanski's folder," Kat explained. "Nick Trotter was your husband, right?"

Helen's brow furrowed as she scanned over the page. "This is for Cherry Hills Veterinary."

"Oh!" Kat smacked her palm against her forehead. "Sorry, I gave you the wrong bill. Let me go get the right one."

She took the invoice from Helen and returned to her car. This time she verified Nick

Trotter's name on the top of the page and the long list of hospital charges before shutting her car door and heading back toward the house.

She only made it halfway up the driveway before a realization hit her so hard she gasped.

She looked down at the bill again, the words 'second notice' printed in red pulling her eyes to the top of the page. She forced her gaze downward, mentally tallying each line item until she finally reached the bottom of the page where the total was printed in bold.

Sherry's words from this morning echoed through her brain. *The charges sure do add up fast, don't they?*

Kat had a flashback of Matty covering up the Furry Friends Foster Families discount on the veterinary invoice that Imogene had given her yesterday. Without a discount, medical charges added up even faster.

Kat lifted her eyes up to Helen's house, her heart slamming against her rib cage. Was it possible that Nick Trotter's medical needs had become so overwhelming that Helen had found herself in a situation where she wasn't able to pay anymore?

The real question was, would such a situation have driven Helen to rob a bank? Kat had to admit, the more she considered the possibility, the more plausible it seemed. Or, was she only scrabbling to assign guilt to someone other than her mother?

Kat thought back to what Jessie had told her about Helen. She'd claimed her aunt loved to talk, that she would practically hold Kat hostage for as long as she was willing to listen to her old stories. Yet Helen had barely said a word yesterday. Kat hadn't given her reticence much thought at the time, too busy catching up with Mrs. Polanski, but what if Helen hadn't been quiet in deference to her sister? What if her reticence was because the topic being discussed had concerned an old crime no one knew she'd committed?

Barely able to feel her own legs, Kat moved toward Helen's house and let herself back inside. Her brain was racing so fast she felt lightheaded. A thousand questions were running through her mind.

"There you are," Helen said. She had settled into the same armchair she had occupied the day before, the Christmas scarf she was knitting in her lap. "I was afraid you'd gotten lost out there."

Kat walked toward the other side of the room in a trance. She was so preoccupied she didn't even check for cats before planting her behind on the sofa.

Helen jerked her chin in Kat's direction. "Is that the bill you were talking about?"

Kat looked at the invoice, almost surprised to see it gripped in her hands. She'd forgotten she was holding it.

She swallowed hard and forced her gaze back up to Helen's. "Yes, it is."

"Thank you for returning it."

"Helen, did you rob that bank?" Kat blurted out.

Helen swayed backward, the force of Kat's question seeming to slam her against the armchair. "What?"

"Did you rob PNW Financial all those years ago?" Kat waved the hospital bill in front of her. "Did your husband's medical treatment get to be so expensive that you no longer had a way to pay for it?"

Helen's mouth gaped open, but no sounds came out. She seemed to be floundering over what to say.

Kat set the invoice on the coffee table and leaned back against the couch. "Helen, I know I could be jumping to conclusions here, but I really need to know the answer. Please. I need to know if you were the one who committed that robbery, the one my mother has been suspected of for the past thirty years."

Helen didn't say anything. Although she'd stopped knitting, the needles clacked together as if she couldn't hold them steady. She looked at them, then set them in her lap.

Shadow jumped onto the vacant couch cushion beside Kat. She stroked the feline to ground herself. "This hospital stay wasn't cheap. And the bill is dated around the same time as the robbery."

Kat waited for Helen to answer, but the only sound in the room was that of Shadow purring.

"You and my mother looked fairly similar back then." Kat eyed the old photograph of Helen and Mrs. Polanski before focusing on Helen again. "I'm not trying to accuse you if you didn't have anything to do with it, but I'm struggling for answers here. If you *did* hold up that bank, I would really, really appreciate you saying something."

Helen dropped her gaze to her lap and started plucking cat furs off of the scarf.

"I wouldn't turn you in," Kat rushed on. "My only interest is to locate my mother. And if I knew she was innocent, I wouldn't need to hide my search from anybody. Besides, the statute of limitations has surely passed if you did have something to do with the bank robbery. I don't think you could be prosecuted even if you went down to the police station and confessed first-hand."

Helen stopped picking at the scarf. "I suppose that's true."

Kat's breath caught. "What exactly is true?"

"About the statute of limitations." Helen swallowed hard and looked up at Kat through lowered eyelids. "And all the rest too."

Kat sucked in a breath, the implications of Helen's statement rocking her to the core. The thought of her mother running from the law for three decades when the real guilty party had been in town all along made her head spin.

"Why?" she whispered.

Helen sighed. "It would help if I started at the beginning. Nick was sick for years. He was always running himself into the ground. I told him to slow down, but that wasn't his nature. He ended up in the hospital on more than one occasion, yet that still didn't deter him. There were times when I thought he was going to die."

"What was wrong with him?" Kat asked.

"Lupus, but it took us years to receive the correct diagnosis." Helen shrugged. "It's bad enough when women get it, but it's even more rare in men. When we finally found a doctor familiar enough with the disease to recognize the symptoms and run the appropriate tests, we were so relieved just to have some answers."

Kat sagged against the couch. The pain on Helen's face inspired a pinch of sympathy in her gut.

Helen stared down at her hands. "I lived every day in fear back then, constantly wondering when Nick would end up in the emergency room next. Then, the times he was admitted, a tiny part of my brain was always questioning whether this would be it, if this would be the last time I would ever see my husband alive."

"And all those hospital visits were expensive," Kat surmised.

A shadow crossed over Helen's face. "Yes. With me being a secretary and him often being too sick to hold down a steady job, it wasn't as if we had great medical insurance or a tremendous source of income."

"So you robbed a bank."

Helen spread her hands. "What other option did I have? Watch Nick suffer at home when I knew he needed to be in the care of professionals?" She shook her head. "That was unconscionable."

Kat's heart twisted as she watched the emotion playing across Helen's face. She didn't envy the decision she'd had to make all those years ago.

"When the idea first came to me, I wasn't sure I would be able to go through with it," Helen continued. "But I had to do something. And I knew I had to choose a bank outside of Cherry Hills, where nobody knew me. So, I started by driving around. I spent some time checking out different establishments. Whenever I'd stop at one, I'd ask myself what I was doing, if I'd lost my mind. Here I was, this law-abiding citizen thinking about committing a major felony."

Helen stopped talking to wipe at the tears pooling around her eyes. Kat turned away for a moment to give her some privacy, only looking back when she started talking again.

"It killed me inside, what I'd been reduced to. Did I really want to be a person who threatened and demanded what wasn't hers?" Helen took a deep breath. "But it always came back to one deciding factor: Nick's health."

"And I'm guessing PNW Financial looked like the easiest target," Kat said.

"Yes. This was back in the eighties, mind you. Security wasn't as good anywhere as it is nowadays, but it struck me as particularly lax at PNW. So I waited until a rainy Tuesday around two, when I figured there would be fewer people, donned a hat and sunglasses to better obscure my face from the cameras, and held up the teller." Helen sighed. "I told her I was armed, but that wasn't really true. I had my hand stuck in my empty jacket pocket the whole time. My heart was pounding so hard, and I had no idea what I would do if she challenged me."

"Did she?"

Helen shook her head. "I don't think it even crossed the poor girl's mind. She was too scared to do anything but hand over the money. Looking back, I believe I was actually more scared than she was, but she didn't know that."

Kat rested one palm on Shadow's soft fur, her stomach clenching as the question she really needed to ask jumped to the forefront of her brain. "How does my mother fit into all this?"

Helen's cheek twisted. "That was rather an unfortunate accident for her. You see, your mama and I, we didn't look so different from a distance, and those grainy films they took in the eighties don't really give you a good look at a person. It didn't help her that I was careful to keep my face down the whole time either."

Kat felt a lump in her throat. "And everybody thought it was my mother in those tapes."

"One of the local cops, a friend of mine, he'd seen the footage. I guess he'd dealt with Maybelle before, when she was picked up for some drug charges. He mentioned how the woman in the tapes looked like her to his superiors, and I gather they ran with it."

A sick feeling settled in Kat's stomach. "And you didn't correct them."

Helen held up her hands. "What was I supposed to do? I couldn't admit I was the one who robbed that bank. Nick needed me. If I went to prison, who would take care of him?"

Kat listed against the couch. "What did my mother do when she realized she was wanted for the robbery?"

Helen pursed her lips. "I guess that's when she fled town. Can't say I blame her. Your mama, I don't want to speak poorly of her, but she didn't have the best reputation. Nobody would have to be strong-armed into believing a person like her would resort to criminal behavior."

Kat felt as if a knife had been shoved into her heart. She could only imagine the dilemma her mother had been put into then. After all, how well would the police have received a protest of innocence from a junkie who had already been deemed unfit to care for her own daughter?

Helen fingered her unfinished scarf. "Over

the years I convinced myself that perhaps everything worked out for the best. Nick got the treatment he needed, and your mama got to escape the bad influences she was exposed to around here and start fresh."

Kat's eyes narrowed. "Except she left me behind."

Helen looked at her, something Kat interpreted as pity reflected in her eyes. "Yes, you were perhaps the one who suffered the most. But can you honestly tell me you would have been better off being raised by a drug addict?"

"That's not the point," Kat spat. She realized her hands were shaking and slipped them between her knees. "You didn't give her a choice."

Helen's face fell. "I know, and I'm truly sorry for that. But what could I do?"

"Start by making things right now."

"How can I do that? It's too late."

"You can tell me where she is."

Helen shook her head. "I can't."

"You owe me."

"Yes, I owe you, but I can't tell you where Maybelle went." Helen's gaze strayed across the room, where two cats had begun tussling. "I don't know the answer. I never knew what happened to her. She just skipped town."

Kat's anger faded, giving way to the suffocating feeling that she wasn't any closer to locating her mother than she had been three days ago.

"I'm sorry," Helen said. "I really would help you find her if I could."

Figuring there was nothing to gain from prolonging this visit, Kat moved Shadow aside and stood up, swallowing past the lump in her throat. "I guess I'll take off then."

Helen set her knitting on the floor and rose from her chair. She took a step forward as if to close the distance between them but then stopped herself. "I really wish I could help you."

Kat looked at her, feeling every inch of the space between them. "I wish you could too."

Helen twined her fingers together. "You mentioned not turning me in earlier."

Kat nodded. "I'll keep my word."

"No." Helen reached her hands out, but they fell back to her sides when Kat retreated. "I don't want you to be burdened by this secret like I've been. Thirty years of silence is long enough. If it helps your search or eases your conscience, go ahead and tell. You have my blessing."

The two women regarded each other for a long moment. Then Kat nodded once and let herself out.

CHAPTER TEN

Kat considered stopping by Cherry Hills Police Department headquarters after leaving Helen's house. But, as anxious as she was to clear her mother's name, she felt too emotionally drained to deal with the authorities. She could talk to Chief Kenny later, after she had more time to process Helen's bombshell.

Instead, she drove straight home and spent the next few hours alternating between bouts of crying and angry cleaning fits. She thought Helen's confession would offer some relief, but she didn't feel any better than she had before. After all, knowing Maybelle hadn't robbed that bank didn't actually bring her back. She had still managed to vanish into thin air, and who knew if Kat would ever get to meet her.

She somehow made it through her evening waitressing shift at Jessie's Diner. By the time she made it home, she was exhausted from engaging in so much small talk. Usually she enjoyed chatting with the restaurant patrons, but today her heart wasn't in it.

Yet, despite being so weary, Kat soon discovered she couldn't sleep. She tossed and turned, pausing occasionally to stroke Tom, who didn't seem bothered by her restlessness. He merely adjusted positions whenever Kat started up with another thrashing bout.

No matter what she did, she couldn't get comfortable. She couldn't stop her mind from going back over every second of her visit to Helen's. Occasionally she would attempt to mold their conversation into something more satisfying by tacking on a made-up ending, one where Helen handed over an address and phone number for Maybelle and broke down sobbing for Kat's forgiveness.

Kat sighed, shaking the fantasy from her head for the hundredth time. Tom rolled over and pressed his back against her thigh. She rested her hand on his warm body, something inside her uncoiling. There really wasn't anything as comforting as a cat.

She must have finally drifted off. When her

doorbell jolted her awake, the morning sun was already shining through the window.

Wrapping a bathrobe around her pajamas and smoothing out her hair using her fingers, Kat padded to the front door. She peered through the peephole, stiffening when she spotted Mrs. Polanski's face looming in front of her. She wasn't in the mood to entertain Helen Trotter's sister after Helen's confession the day before.

Kat drew herself up and opened the door. "Hi, Mrs. Polanski. What are you doing here?"

"Jess gave me your address, and one of your neighbors let me into the building. I thought it would be better to talk to you in person than to call." Mrs. Polanski smiled, but it was a more subdued version of the beaming grin that normally usurped her entire face. "Helen told me about your visit yesterday."

Kat's grip tightened around the doorknob. She didn't know what to say to that.

Mrs. Polanski shifted her weight to her other foot. "May I come in?"

Kat considered telling her that she really needed to be alone right now, but relented when she saw the earnest look on Mrs. Polanski's face. Nodding, she swung the door open and stepped aside.

Tom's eyes lit up when he spotted their guest. He meowed a greeting, rushed over, and flopped onto the floor in front of them, holding his front legs above his head in order to expose his stomach.

Mrs. Polanski laughed as she reached down and scratched the big cat's belly. "Well, aren't you a friendly fella."

"That's Tom," Kat told her, closing the door.

Kat couldn't help but relax a little as she watched Tom basking in Mrs. Polanski's attention. She could always trust Tom to cut the tension of an awkward situation.

After petting Tom for a minute, Mrs. Polanski straightened, her amused look fading into one of worry as her eyes drifted toward Kat. "I came to see how you were dealing with everything."

Kat sat down on the sofa and twisted her hands in her lap. "As well as can be expected, I guess."

Mrs. Polanski glanced at the empty couch across from Kat. "May I sit down?"

"Sure."

Kat studied Mrs. Polanski as she settled into the sofa. Something in her expression spurred a tingling sensation in the back of Kat's brain. She wasn't sure why, but it reminded her of the look

Mrs. Polanski had given Helen when the subject of PNW Financial had been brought up. Looking back, maybe the look didn't reflect her belief in Maybelle's guilt so much as her knowledge of Helen's secret.

The possibility sent Kat's mind reeling. Could it be that Mrs. Polanski had known about her sister's crime all these years? The more Kat considered it, the more plausible it seemed. She could tell the two were close from the way they had their arms thrown around each other in that photograph, the pure joy reflected on their faces captured for the rest of eternity. And who better to hide your darkest secret than a trusted sibling?

Kat collapsed against the couch. Viewing Mrs. Polanski in such a shocking new light had drained every last ounce of strength from her body. "You knew, didn't you?"

"Yes."

Kat was surprised by the quick admission. She had feared she would need to pry whatever Mrs. Polanski knew out of her. "Why didn't you say anything?"

Mrs. Polanski crossed her ankles. "It wasn't my place."

Kat processed that. "Did you help her?"

Mrs. Polanski covered her chest with one

hand. "Heavens, no. Helen didn't even want to tell me what she did at first, but I can put two and two together. I might not be a genius, but I know my sister like the back of my hand."

"Did you know she let one of her police officer friends believe my mother was guilty?"

Mrs. Polanski's eyes dimmed. "I did."

Kat had to ungrit her teeth in order to respond. "And you didn't say anything."

"How could I? Helen is my own flesh and blood." Mrs. Polanski sighed. "I always felt guilty about that, you know. Remember all those milkshakes I used to give you on the house?"

Kat's jaw dropped open. Her lungs suddenly felt too small. "You gave those to me out of guilt?"

"Yes. I'm sorry to say it, but I did."

Before Kat could reply, Matty came sprinting into the room. The rambunctious feline vaulted on top of the coffee table, sending the folder of newspaper clippings skittering to the floor. She flattened her ears against her skull and wiggled her rear end before leaping into the center of the pile.

Kat jumped off the sofa. "Matty!"

Matty froze, her huge green eyes rotating toward Kat as her tail cut through the air.

Mrs. Polanski leaned forward. “Are those the articles I gave you?”

“Yes.” Kat plucked one off the floor and smoothed it out.

“Did you read through them all?”

“I did.” Kat grabbed a few more articles, trying to collect what she could before Matty destroyed them all.

Tom wandered over to see what the commotion was about, his tail puffed up to the size of a feather duster. He sniffed at the edge of one of the pages before extending a tentative paw.

Matty, however, wasn’t nearly so cautious. She slapped at one of the clippings as Kat tried to stack it with the others. Kat had to laugh at the look of determination in the feline’s eyes, but she cut herself off mid-chuckle. Although she was upset enough with Mrs. Polanski to not care if the cats ruined her newspaper collection, a part of her also didn’t want Mrs. Polanski thinking she didn’t appreciate her willingness to help.

“Give that to me, Matty.” Kat tried to lift her paw, but Matty resisted, digging her claws into the newsprint.

Kat’s eyes traveled down the length of Matty’s leg to where she had her toes planted in the center of Kelly Watson’s obituary, the one

Mrs. Polanski had circled.

Matty released the obituary in order to pounce on some of the other clippings, running around in circles as she bounced from article to article. She seemed to get a kick out of the crinkling sound created by her activity. Either that or she enjoyed shocking Tom as he watched her with rounded eyes.

Kat glanced at Mrs. Polanski as she set the obituary on top of her makeshift pile. "Did you know Kelly Watson?"

Mrs. Polanski shook her head. "No, I did not."

"You were friends with her parents?" Kat guessed.

"No, I didn't know them either."

Kat frowned. She was about to ask why Mrs. Polanski had saved the obituary in that case when she felt her gaze being drawn back to the write-up.

Her brain tingled as she stared at the faded outline of the hand-drawn circle around the succinct summary of Kelly Watson's short life. Her mother would have been about twenty-seven back in 1985, the same age as Kelly.

Kat gripped the newspaper clipping in both hands and sat back down on the couch, her head spinning. Was it possible that her mother had stolen this woman's identity? Stealing an existing identity would certainly be easier than establishing a fake social security number and everything else needed to live in the United States. She would only have to apply for a copy of the woman's birth certificate, or have one forged, and use the dead woman's information to obtain all the other documents she needed.

Kat looked up at Mrs. Polanski. Her mouth had gone dry, and she had to work to get her next question out. "Did you help my mother hide out?"

"You figured it out from the death announcement, didn't you?" When Kat nodded, Mrs. Polanski leaned back, looking satisfied. "I knew you would. You always were a smart one."

Kat didn't know what to say to that. At the moment she didn't feel very smart. She felt as if the joke was on her.

"It was easier than I thought it would be," Mrs. Polanski said, fingering the edge of her shirt. "Turning Maybelle Harper into Kelly Watson, that is."

Kat mustered up some saliva and swallowed. "Yeah?"

"Finding somebody willing to work fast to create the fake ID was the most difficult part. After that, I only had to lend her the money for an apartment and provide her with a good reference so Country Eats would hire her."

Kat took a deep breath, trying to tamp down the mix of emotions coursing through her. "Why didn't you just tell me?"

Mrs. Polanski spread her hands. "In front of Helen?"

Kat's eyes widened. "She doesn't know?"

Mrs. Polanski shook her head. "If she had been paying attention back then I'm sure she would have seen I was up to something. Helen knows me as well as I know her. But after the robbery she was too wrapped up in her own thoughts. So, everything I did for Maybelle stayed between her and me."

Kat shook the newspaper in her hand, struggling to understand. "But you gave me all these articles, hoping I put everything together."

Mrs. Polanski's eyes softened. "You have a right to know about your mama. And I didn't figure you would turn her in once you realized what name she was using. That would only jeopardize her freedom. Until Helen's crime came to light, it wasn't safe for Maybelle to reveal herself either."

Kat absorbed that. She didn't know for sure if what Mrs. Polanski was saying was true. She didn't figure she could keep such a huge secret from Andrew, who in turn might be duty-bound to notify Chief Kenny.

Kat watched Matty and Tom playing with the newspaper clippings, needing a moment to corral her thoughts. She knew she should stop the cats before they made too much of a mess, but she felt paralyzed by what she'd just learned.

"So, when are you going to call her?" Mrs. Polanski asked.

Kat turned to face her. "I don't have her number."

Mrs. Polanski flapped her hand. "She'd be easy enough to locate with directory assistance."

"She might not even live in Estacada anymore. And what if she's married now, with a new family? What if she . . ." Kat trailed off, not wanting to ask out loud the question that still haunted her. *What if she doesn't want to hear from me?*

"Well, you're not going to get answers to any of those questions unless you pick up the phone, now are you?" Mrs. Polanski reached for Kat's cell phone on the coffee table and held it out.

Kat stared at it, a flare of terror searing her chest. Now that she was so close to finding her mother, her insecurities had returned in full force.

Mrs. Polanski sighed. "She didn't want to leave you, you know."

Kat's eyes snapped toward hers. "She didn't?"

"No. She asked me if I thought she should take you with her." Mrs. Polanski closed her eyes for a moment. "I said I couldn't imagine leaving Jessie behind if I were in her situation, but I also wouldn't want to expose my daughter to the type of life that comes with running from the law. Plus, she still had all that drug business she was trying to shake. She knew, no matter how much she loved you, that that wasn't the life she wanted you to have."

"So she opted to abandon me," Kat said, hearing how dull her own voice sounded.

Mrs. Polanski shook her head. "She opted to let you go if that meant you would have a better life than the one she could give you."

Tears burned behind Kat's eyes, and she blinked them away. Somehow, she'd never considered that walking away might have been difficult for her mother. It had never occurred to her that Maybelle had only left her because she loved Kat so much she was willing to put her own needs aside for those of her child.

Mrs. Polanski thrust the phone closer.

"Here. Call directory assistance. It's past time that your mama stopped running, and you should be the one to tell her she no longer has to hide."

Kat stared at Mrs. Polanski's outstretched hand for a moment longer. Then she took a deep breath, accepted the phone, and dialed.

CHAPTER ELEVEN

"So, you finally got to talk to her, huh?" Andrew asked, taking Kat's hand as they walked through the parking lot toward the police station.

Kat smiled. "I did. The conversation didn't go at all like I expected, but it was good."

He looked at her, his eyes warm. "Yeah?"

"I always figured we'd either have this big, tearful heart-to-heart or she'd tell me she never wanted to hear from me again." Kat paused, then said, "This wasn't like either scenario."

In fact, after Kat had pushed past her initial nervousness, talking to her mother for the first time in three decades almost felt like chatting with a customer at Jessie's Diner. There were no huge displays of emotion from either party, but just hearing that twinge of excitement in her mother's voice when Kat had revealed who she was had been enough.

"She wants to meet me," Kat said.

"She'd be a fool not to," Andrew replied.

She stopped walking and turned to face him. "I'm not sure I'm ready."

He took her other hand, not saying anything.

She looked off in the distance, her heart hammering in her chest. She wasn't sure how to explain her hesitation. She had yearned so badly for a reunion a week ago, back before she had any method of contacting her mother. Now that they'd actually spoken, she was more unsure than ever.

"I mean, I want to meet her," Kat said, her eyes drifting back to Andrew. "I just need some time to get used to the idea before we actually go through with it."

Andrew squeezed her fingers. "That's your right."

He let go of one of her hands, but maintained his grip on the other as they started walking again. Kat looked up at the sky, watching as two clouds glided past each other. When they separated, the sun appeared, casting its warm rays down upon them.

Kat turned back to Andrew. "We agreed to keep the lines of communication open. We're going to call each other every week or so, just to catch up. Maybe after we've talked for a while I'll feel more comfortable with the idea of meeting her in person."

"Whatever you do, I'll support you."

Her heart warmed. "I know, and I'm so grateful you feel that way."

Andrew released her hand to open the door to the police station. "After you."

Kat stepped inside, her stomach executing a nervous flip as they headed toward Chief Kenny's office. She wasn't sure how he would react to the information she had to share.

But Chief Kenny let her talk freely as she told him about Helen Trotter's confession, interrupting only when he needed clarification on certain points. And although Andrew had accompanied her into the police chief's office, he merely sat quietly in one corner, observing but not participating.

Kat omitted any mention of Mrs. Polanski and what she'd done to help Maybelle hide from the law. She didn't think the police chief would look very favorably on her mother's decision to take on another woman's identity, even given the circumstances.

Plus, now that the shock of what she'd learned had worn off, Kat felt oddly grateful to Mrs. Polanski for helping her mother out all those years ago. Clearly turning Helen in would have helped Maybelle even more, but Kat could understand—begrudgingly—why that hadn't been an option.

Kat took a deep breath when she reached the end of her story. "So, that's it. Now that you know my mother is innocent, you can remove her from your wanted list, right?"

Chief Kenny folded his bulky arms on the desk. If he was surprised by Helen's guilt, his face didn't reflect it. "I still want to see her," he said.

Kat's heart lurched. "Why? Helen's confession is enough to prove my mother had nothing to do with that robbery, right?"

"You betcha," Chief Kenny said, nodding. His head stilled, and his face fell a little. "I wanna apologize for suspecting her all these years."

Kat stared at him for a moment. As uncomfortable as the police chief had made her at the end of their first meeting, now she felt something bordering on warmth. She knew it took a lot of courage for someone in his position to admit to being wrong.

She swallowed. “If she ever comes back to Cherry Hills, I’ll be sure to let her know.”

Chief Kenny shook his head. “*When* she comes back, Kat, even if it’s just for a short visit, tell her she’ll be welcome with open arms.”

Kat smiled. “I’ll do that.”

She was still smiling when she walked out of the police station.

NOTE FROM THE AUTHOR

Thank you for visiting Cherry Hills, home of Kat, Matty, and Tom! If you enjoyed their story, please consider leaving a book review on your favorite retailer and/or review site.

Keep reading for an excerpt from Book Five of the Cozy Cat Caper Mystery series, *Shot in Cherry Hills*, and descriptions of some of the other books in the series. Thank you!

SHOT *in* CHERRY HILLS

Animal rescue with a side of murder.

What starts off as a foster dog wellness check turns into a nightmare when a gunshot leads Kat Harper to a man's dead body. Eric Halstead's killer is gone by the time Kat arrives on the scene, but the amateur sleuth isn't about to let them get away that easily.

By all accounts, this homicide appears to be a neighborhood dispute turned deadly. And now it's up to Kat to determine exactly which neighbor pulled the trigger. Was it the do-it-yourself handyman who didn't appreciate Eric's frequent noise complaints? Or could it have been the local newspaper thief who swears he knows something relevant to the murder but refuses to talk to the police? And Kat certainly can't discount the loudmouthed older gentleman who seems to have a not-always-popular opinion about everything.

Kat might not know "whodunit" yet, but she knows one thing for sure. There's a lot more than justice riding on this case. With Eric's death comes the need to rehome his beloved tuxedo cat. And if Kat's not careful, this animal rescue mission may end with the newly orphaned feline falling into the hands of a cold-blooded killer.

* * *

Please check your favorite online retailer for availability.

Excerpt From

SHOT *in* CHERRY HILLS

PAIGE SLEUTH

"What exactly happens during a wellness check?" Katherine Harper asked, looking across the console at Imogene Little.

Imogene kept her gaze trained out the windshield, her hands in perfect ten-and-two position on the steering wheel. "We make sure the foster animal is faring well in his temporary environment, and the foster parents have everything they need."

Kat leaned back in the passenger seat, savoring the crisp fall breeze as it hit her face through the open window. "Sounds simple enough."

"Oh, it is. It's mainly a way to let everybody know we're here if they need anything."

Kat smiled as she watched the wind whip

Imogene's auburn hair around her face. Since volunteering to serve as treasurer of the Furry Friends Foster Families nonprofit organization in July, her admiration for Imogene had only grown. She had always liked the 4F president, but in the past three months she'd really gotten to witness firsthand how much she cared about animals and was willing to work on their behalf. It made her proud to be a part of 4F.

Kat's gaze drifted out the windshield, landing on the large dog standing next to a woman in front of one of the two-story houses lining this street. She sat up a little straighter. "There's Champ."

"That sure is." Imogene turned into the driveway. "He looks well. Noreen must be taking good care of him."

Kat presumed the woman was Noreen. She was a petite blonde who looked to be around Imogene's age, somewhere in her fifties. Her trim figure and healthy tan suggested she spent a lot of time outdoors.

She held a retractable leash in one hand, letting out some of the pull as Champ snuffled the ground. But the grass lost its appeal when Champ saw Imogene's car. He looked up, his tail wagging fast enough to make Kat dizzy.

Kat climbed out of the passenger seat. With

the car engine off, she could hear birds chirping up in the trees. She grinned, imagining them taking shelter on the uppermost branches as they warned their companions of the big dog down on the ground.

Champ's ears pricked, and he trotted over to Kat. She rubbed his head, her heart soaring at how happy he looked. He'd had a traumatic time a couple months ago, and she was glad to see the experience hadn't broken him.

Champ nudged her hip with his head. She took a step back, laughing as she pushed him away.

"Hello to you too," she said. "You'll notice I remembered to wear jeans instead of a dress around you."

The blonde walked over. "He likes you."

Kat grinned. "The feeling is mutual."

"I'm Noreen Wilkenson." She stuck her leash-free hand out.

"Kat Harper."

As if he wanted to take part in the formal introduction, Champ barked before pressing his nose against their joined palms.

Noreen broke off the handshake to scratch Champ between the ears. "This one is going to make somebody very happy. I tried to convince Stacey Whitfield from two doors down to adopt him, but she says she has her hands full just with Vern."

"What kind of dog is Vern?" Kat asked.

"The worst." Noreen snorted. "He's her husband. He likes to start on home improvement projects, but he doesn't like to finish them. Stacey is trying to cure him of that."

On cue, the sound of what Kat guessed to be an electric saw cut through the air. Champ turned toward it and barked.

"And, that would be Vern," Noreen said with a grimace. "I swear he's getting worse. He used to only work on his projects on Saturdays, but now that it's cooling down there's no predicting when he'll be out in the garage."

Imogene tilted her face to the sky, the sunlight catching her hair at an angle that made it look as if it were on fire. "The weather's been so nice, I don't blame him."

"There's no better place to be in October than Cherry Hills, Washington," Noreen agreed, running her hand down Champ's back.

Champ gazed up at her with adoring eyes before giving her hand a lick.

Noreen bent over and planted a kiss on top of the dog's head. "Oh, baby, I love you too."

Kat's heart melted. If it weren't for her two cats and small apartment, she would be tempted to adopt Champ herself.

Noreen looked at Kat. "Would you like to hold the reins while you're here?"

"Sure." Kat took the leash from her.

The power saw shut off. Before Kat could adjust to the quiet, a bang loud enough for her to feel it in her teeth echoed through the air. She jumped, losing her hold on the leash and having to retrieve it from the grass with shaky fingers.

A couple of nearby birds squawked before flying off. Kat could hear the blood rushing through her ears in the silence they left behind.

She set one hand on Champ, feeling the tenseness of his muscles beneath her palm. His tail was no longer moving. Now he stood stock-still, his ears rotated at attention. His reaction made the hairs on the back of Kat's neck stand up.

"What was that?" Imogene asked, her voice wavering.

Noreen's eyes were wide. The tan Kat had admired only a moment earlier had disappeared, replaced now by a complexion that bordered on ashen.

"I'm not sure," Noreen said slowly, "but it sounded like a gunshot."

* * *

Please check your favorite online retailer for availability.

STRANGLED *in* CHERRY HILLS

Three cats, two dogs, and one dead body.

Kat Harper isn't the only one with a knack for stumbling upon crime scenes. This time she's led to the corpse du jour by her adventurous cat Matty and one determined dachshund. It doesn't take long before the dead man is identified as local dog walker Jeffrey Parr—and his doxie client could be the only eyewitness to this latest Cherry Hills homicide.

Kat doesn't set out to investigate, but what can she do when the task of reuniting the dachshund with his owner introduces her to more suspects than she can count? Between Jeffrey's disgruntled clients and his angry exes, Kat has her hands full trying to determine "whodunit." That might be a blessing in disguise though. As the amateur sleuth soon learns, success often comes with a price. And when Kat finds herself in the killer's crosshairs, it might just be up to her furry feline friends to save her from becoming the next murder victim.

* * *

Please check your favorite online retailer for availability.

HALLOWEEN *in* CHERRY HILLS

Halloween has arrived in Cherry Hills, Washington—the worst time of the year for a black cat to disappear.

Coming home to discover a beloved fur baby has gone missing is every pet parent's worst nightmare. But that's exactly what happens to Cherry Hills High School teacher Tracy Montgomery. The question is, did Midnight escape, or was he catnapped?

With all evidence suggesting the friendly black cat didn't sneak out on his own, Kat Harper and her fellow Furry Friends Foster Families animal rescue volunteers take it upon themselves to locate the elusive feline and reunite him with his frantic owner. Unfortunately, their only leads turn out to be a scrap of paper and the neighborhood witch's cryptic vision. But the lack of clues isn't going to deter Kat. Halloween is fast approaching, and giving up now could very well mean letting an animal thief triumph.

* * *

Please check your favorite online retailer for availability.

STABBED *in* CHERRY HILLS

Job hunting can be murder.

Kat Harper wants nothing more than to forget about her disastrous job interview, but that's pretty hard to do when your interviewer turns up dead. Now Kat's search for employment has turned into a search for a killer.

As Kat soon discovers, she has her work cut out for her. Leo Price left behind quite a few enemies, including a struggling former business partner and a bevy of ex-girlfriends. But the amateur sleuth isn't going to let the abundance of suspects discourage her. While she labors to find temporary accommodations for Stumpy, Leo's gray Manx cat, she's also sniffing out as many clues as she can. She'd better hope the wrong person doesn't catch wind of her investigation though, or it may be up to her furry feline pals to save her from tragedy once more.

* * *

Please check your favorite online retailer for availability.

ABOUT THE AUTHOR

Paige Sleuth is a pseudonym for mystery author Marla Bradeen. She plots murder during the day and fights for mattress space with her two rescue cats at night. When not attending to her cats' demands, she writes. Find her at: http://www.marlabradeen.com

CPSIA information can be obtained
at www.ICGtesting.com
Printed in the USA
LVHW090420160621
690365LV00012B/186